Praise for *Hope the Hopeful Piglet*

"This short and beautiful story is the kind of stories I believe parents should be sharing with their babies, the next generation, who has a power to change how we view life and our perception of other animals. Hope's story is one that many animals have experienced, but unfortunately, many more have experienced the story of her mother. It is the both the responsibility and the privilege of parents to raise kids who will try their best to take important moral stances and live ethical lives. In a world where many ignore the importance of concepts such as love and respect, let Hope's story raise children who will embrace these concepts."—**Seb Alex**, animal rights activist, lecturer, photojournalist, and author

"All libraries need to make space on their shelves for *Hope the Hopeful Piglet* and her story. Told through the eyes of this adorable little pig, children will be gently educated and entertained by her moving story. I truly wish this book existed back when I was a kid."—**Sorsha Morava**, animal rights activist and content creator

"The book I wish I read as a child! A wonderful introduction into animal rights… A thoughtful, heartfelt, realistic, and compassionate look at the animals that children love."—**Atomic Vegans**, animal rights activists and artists

"A little story of Hope, her life was almost lost.
People wanted to hurt her; they didn't know the cost.
She's such a smart, loving girl who, like us, can think and feel.
How ever could we hurt her, she's more than just a meal."
—**Emma Graf**, animal rights activist and mother

"The hardest part about raising vegan children isn't what to feed them; It's protecting their natural sense of compassion in a world full of indifference."
—**Sara Marti**, animal rights activist and mother

"For too many it's easy to turn a blind eye to the voiceless victims of animal agriculture. This uplifting tale lends a voice to one such victim and pulls at our heartstrings as we experience the realities of our cruel food system from a baby animal's point of view. As a mother, I couldn't help but empathize with the main character as if she were my own little one. It's essential to educate kids about everyday injustices like this and empower them to make compassionate choices for animals, people, and the planet."—**Ashley Renne Nsonwu**, activist, speaker, educator

"This book beautifully illustrates how all animals are the same—they all want love happiness companionship and freedom. Unfortunately, today's society teaches our children that some animals are to be protected and loved, and some are to be imprisoned and hurt. It's so important to re-educate our future generations that all animals are equal and deserve to live their lives in peace. That's why as activists we need to spread the word of veganism, for the good of the animals, our planet, and also our own health."—**Sarah Jane Abdennadher**, animal rights activist

Hope the Hopeful Piglet

A Picture Book Teaching Children Kindness and Compassion

Written by Devin Staurbringer
Illustrated by Emily N. B.

Inspired by Sunfish/Sable from Compassion Over Cruelty

Lantern Publishing & Media • Woodstock & Brooklyn, NY

2023
Lantern Publishing & Media
PO Box 1350
Woodstock, NY 12498
www.lanternpm.org

Printed in the United States of America

Library of Congress Cataloging-in-Publication Data

Names: Staubringer, Devin, author. | Buford, Emily, illustrator.
Title: Hope the hopeful piglet : teaching children kindness and compassion / written by Devin Staubringer ; illustrated by Emily Buford.
Description: Woodstock and Brooklyn, NY : Lantern Publishing & Media, 2023. | Audience: Grades 2-3. | Summary: Hope, a baby piglet born on a factory farm, is very scared and sad, but one night a little girl comes into the dark building and takes Hope to a farm where humans love the animals and give them hugs.
Identifiers: LCCN 2022030613 (print) | LCCN 2022030614 (ebook) | ISBN 9781590566923 (hardcover) | ISBN 9781590566930 (epub)
Subjects: CYAC: Pigs—Fiction. | Animals—Infancy—Fiction. | Hope—Fiction. | Compassion—Fiction.
Classification: LCC PZ7.1.S7384 Ho 2023 (print) | LCC PZ7.1.S7384 (ebook) | DDC [E]—dc23
LC record available at https://lccn.loc.gov/2022030613
LC ebook record available at https://lccn.loc.gov/2022030614

This book is dedicated to all the past, present, and future vegans who make the world a kinder and happier place for all.

Foreword

Some pigs love snuggles, as much as your dog loves cuddles.

And piglets love to play just like puppies, by the way.

They all want your love; can you give them some?

They're not bacon, ham, or a sandwich for eating.

They're smart, beautiful animals with a heart that's beating.

Once you meet them, you can't eat them.

So, until then, just eat something vegan instead.

I have been an animal rights activist and a vegan for over 13 years, and I'm happy to see this beautiful children's book.

I have visited pig farms all over the world to see the horrible situations these amazing animals are in, and on the other side, I've visited animal sanctuaries all over the world, and spent quality time with pigs rescued from these places.

Pigs, just like all animals, have unique, interesting personalities, I'm privileged to have had quality time with pigs who escaped animal agriculture. No animal deserves to be born only to be eaten in a sandwich.

This book shows how we love dogs, but we treat other animals so badly. It shows us that they all deserve to be loved, and that no animal should be treated badly simply because of their species.

If you are already vegan, thank you.

If you aren't vegan, please, show that you are a real animal lover, and go vegan today.

David Ramms,
animal rights videographer, photographer, content creator and public speaker

My name is Hope, and I am a piglet.

My mommy named me Hope
before she was taken away.

Today I think I'm going on an adventure!

Maybe I'm going to where mommy went!

My piglet friends and I
were put on to a big truck.

It's hot and smelly in here, but it will be worth
it once we get to wherever we're going.

I stuck my face out of a hole so that I could get fresh air,
and then there came a bird flying next to the truck.

"Hi bird! Where are you going?" I asked.
"Hi there! I'm flying to the park." The bird replied.
I was confused and asked, "What is the park?"

The bird said, "It's a wonderful place with green grass and many animal friends."

"That sounds lovely, I hope I'm going to the park too. Goodbye friend!" I replied.

Then the truck stopped moving. A car came next to us, and inside was a dog.

"Hi dog!" I exclaimed.
"Hi there!" The dog said.
"Where are you going?" I asked.
"To the beach." He replied.
"What is the beach?" I asked curiously.

The dog told me, "It's a beautiful place, filled with blue waves of water and a fresh breeze!"

"Wow, that sounds special, I hope I'm
going to the beach!" I said.
Then the truck started to move, and I
told my dog friend goodbye.

The truck stopped outside of a big building. I saw
a squirrel in a tree, so I said, "Hi there squirrel!"
She said, "Hello friend!"

"Where are you going?" I asked her.
"I'm going to the forest!" She said.
"What is the forest?" I asked with wonder.

"It's a magical place, with big green trees and lots of animals of all kinds." She said. "Oh my! That does sound magical! I hope I'm going to the forest too!" I exclaimed.

Once the truck started to move again,
I said goodbye to my squirrel friend.
The truck drove into the big building.

CAUTION

MEAT
and
PROCESSING

23

But this place doesn't look like the park, no green grass.
And it doesn't feel like the beach, no fresh breeze.
And it doesn't sound like the forest, no animal friends.

My piglet friends and I were put in cages,
and strangers took some of my friends away.
My friends never came back. And I heard the men say,
"You'll make some tasty bacon."
I don't know what bacon is, but it doesn't sound very nice.

BACON

I sat there for many days and nights. I can't even count the days because I never saw the sun, only darkness. Sometimes there was light when they opened the door to take more of my friends away.

Then one night, a human came in dressed all in black with a black mask. They picked me up and said, "We're going to get you out of here little one."

They put me in a car and took off their mask. It was a beautiful little girl! We drove all night and arrived at a new place in the early morning.

Here they have green grass like the park,
and blue water like the beach, and big trees like the forest.

And there are lots and lots of animal friends to meet! I'm friends with cows, chickens, sheep, horses, cats, dogs, and even more pigs like me! And every day more animal friends show up.

My friends all have similar stories to me.
They told me how they were rescued from dark, scary places.
And they told me that they were brought here to the nice, happy
place. A place where humans give lots of food, lots of play time,
and lots of cuddles and love.

I am so happy here. Now I know why my mommy named me Hope. Because I hope all animals of all kinds get rescued and get to live a fun and happy life.

THE END

Every life is precious to the one living it.
A kinder world begins with you.

About the Author

Devin Staurbringer is a writer and activist. He is passionate about helping animals, people, and the planet. He has been vegan for over 10 years, loves writing, photography, and nature. As well as writing, Devin is also currently posting educational and humorous vegan related videos on his Instagram, @vegan.activist.devin He hopes to travel the world while writing and working in activism, bringing compassion wherever he goes.

About the Illustrator

Emily N. B. is a Latina illustrator and graphic designer based in California. She has worked with organizations such as *Vegan F.T.A* and *Animal Rebellion*. She works on spreading kindness and compassion for animals with her illustrations on Instagram, (@soy._.emily). She is new to her profession, but she has been a passionate artist and animal rights advocate since she was a child.

About the Publisher

Lantern Publishing & Media was founded in 2020 to follow and expand on the legacy of Lantern Books—a publishing company started in 1999 on the principles of living with a greater depth and commitment to the preservation of the natural world. Like its predecessor, Lantern Publishing & Media produces books on animal advocacy, veganism, religion, social justice, humane education, psychology, family therapy, and recovery. Lantern is dedicated to printing in the United States on recycled paper and saving resources in our day-to-day operations. Our titles are also available as ebooks and audiobooks.

To catch up on Lantern's publishing program, visit us at www.lanternpm.org.

facebook.com/lanternpm
instagram.com/lanternpm
twitter.com/lanternpm